THIS BOOK BELONGS TO:

This book is dedicated to all of the wonderful fathers, grandfathers, uncles, brothers and godfathers. You do not receive enough credit for how much of an impact you are in your child/children's lives. Not only is a solid support system, affection & interaction vital in a child's life, it is life changing in regards to one's social development. It also has a major impact on one's cognitive skills. Dedicated fathers, the love you give does not go unnoticed.

Just Like
MY
DAD

Just like my dad,
I am strong.

Family
grateful thankful blessed

Just like my dad,
I pray.

My dad teaches me right from wrong.
He expresses to me that crying is okay.
Crying does not make you weak.
Crying does not make you less of a man.
Crying indicates that you have emotions.
The freedom of expression
should be conveyed.

BORN
LEADER
READING
IS
FUNDAMENTAL

Just like my dad, I am smart.
I like to gain knowledge by reading.
Reading is fundamental
and broadens horizons.
I like to read at least one book a day.

OMG!
WOW
Follow You
Dreams
OK
BANG
!!!

Just like my dad, I want to teach.
I want to teach what he taught me.
Educating oneself leads to success,
prosperity and learning day by day.

Just like my dad, I am Superman.
I am a hero with a cape.
I will lead the pack instead of following,
similar to how
Martin Luther King Jr. paved the way.

Just like my dad, I am a leader standing tall.
I am a reflection of him, so I will not fall.
I have a superhero for a dad, so giving up
does not exist. He holds my hand
through it all, just in case I trip.

Dad taught me how to ride a bike.
Dad taught me how to skip.
Dad taught me how to tie my shoes
so that I never ever slip.

Now I am a pro! I told him to watch me go.
Go faster and faster and faster
since I mastered what I know.

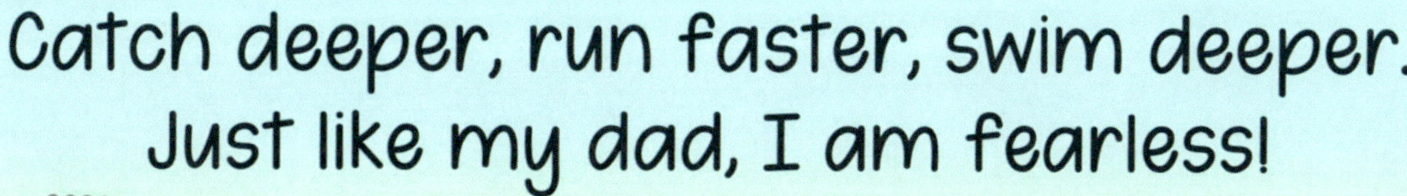

Catch deeper, run faster, swim deeper.
Just like my dad, I am fearless!

Superheroes do exist.
My superhero`s name is Dad!

Just like My Dad

Crossword Puzzle

s	t	o	o	b	f	e	a	r	n	b	k	u
u	z	f	k	m	u	l	m	o	l	h	n	s
p	s	t	r	o	n	g	s	q	p	j	o	l
e	u	z	e	y	d	a	d	u	i	o	w	q
r	p	b	f	n	a	e	t	x	e	p	l	s
m	e	v	l	t	m	q	w	a	c	s	e	t
a	r	h	e	h	e	r	o	d	j	u	d	r
n	h	i	c	t	n	f	w	e	c	x	g	i
z	e	k	t	v	t	b	z	g	a	t	e	v
b	r	q	i	k	a	g	x	i	p	e	n	e
c	o	z	o	m	l	e	a	d	e	r	e	y
n	f	b	n	q	f	e	a	r	l	e	s	s
v	t	m	c	r	d	i	z	i	o	a	w	f
h	p	a	p	r	e	k	a	k	s	d	t	z

Dad	Superhero	Leader	Fundamental
Hero	Cape	Strong	Reflection
Superman	Fearless	Knowledge	Read

Write a Sentence

Directions: Write a sentence using the words from the word bank below & cross off each word as you use it.

Dad	superhero	leader	fundamental
hero	cape	strong	reflection
superman	fearless	knowledge	read

1 ____________________
2 ____________________
3 ____________________
4 ____________________
5 ____________________
6 ____________________
7 ____________________
8 ____________________
9 ____________________
10 ____________________
11 ____________________
12 ____________________

Made in the USA
Columbia, SC
26 July 2025

60821275R00015